The Undergrowth

Also by Robert Horne and published by Ginninderra Press

Love the Hurt

Robert Horne

The Undergrowth

& other stories

The Undergrowth & other stories
ISBN 978 1 74027 276 6
Copyright © Robert Horne 2004

First published 2004
Reprinted 2017

GINNINDERRA PRESS
PO Box 3461 Port Adelaide 5015
www.ginninderrapress.com.au

Contents

A Practice in the Suburbs

'Well, what do you know?' Alex sometimes twisted Australian turns of phrase to his work mates as part of the Friday-night ritual at the pub. It was his way of clawing back a point or two from his Anglo colleagues. Tonight he used an exaggerated lick of Greek accent, a kind of self-parody, dipping the hat to his long-struggling parents.

'Well, a few things I guess.' Simon was more reserved than normal and pursed his lips thoughtfully. He pushed his West End slightly away from him and looked after the arse of the bar girl as she disappeared around the corner into the front bar.

'Not bad, that,' and Simon raised his eyebrows and jagged his head in the direction of the corner around which the girl had disappeared, but all Alex could see now was a group of off-duty firemen from the station across the road, drinking pints and talking loudly, chins like jetties and meaty mitts covering their beers almost entirely.

'You've changed over,' Alex nodded in their direction.

'I think I'll leave the fireys to my unmentionable uncle Bertie.'

'Of course! The famous queer magistrate whom you manage to mention regularly. Pity my family are just hard-working Greeks. Not worth the breath it takes to mention them, really.'

But there the banter lapsed quickly, unaccustomedly, and Alex noticed signs of tension around Simon's eyes.

Simon exhaled his Benson and Hedges and turned around to face the opaque saloon bar window. No one could see out, no one could see in, a sealed environment until you stepped outside and into the cold June evening. Perhaps this was the best place to do it, just like old McBride had said. But Simon had never been convinced, and Simon was no hero.

'You do know something,' Alex drummed his fingers on the bar in a comical exaggeration of impatience, 'and you're going to tell me in a minute. It's about the partnership, isn't it?'

Simon focused on the television behind the bar; Lillee was bowling – the comeback Lillee, post major back injury: streamlined, efficient and accurate. Not the hair flying, elbows-out larrikin of his early days. From his distance in the back of the members' stand, Simon had liked the old Lillee rather than this spruced up and trimmed down eighties' version.

He wished he'd had ten beers now instead of one and a half. He still needed something to get him over the big hurdles. This was something he would rather have fumbled from his mouth late at night, at about midnight, stumbling out of the Trat after a saltimbocca and a full bottle of red – muffled, slurred, desensitised – then home to bed and sleep and forget. But Alex and he only ever had the two drinks after work, Fridays only.

The problem in the cricket seemed to be a big, dark left-hander with a bushy moustache and a white crash helmet.

'That's Lloyd.' Alex showed off his limited cricket knowledge. 'He's too cagey for your mate Lillee. Now have I ever told you about this ancient guy Themistocles who saved the Greeks from the Persians about two and a half thousand years ago? Now there was a tactician.'

'Acchh!' Simon exhaled scornfully. He had heard about Themistocles a hundred times.

'What's up, Simon? Jesus!'

Simon stubbed out his fag, ordered another beer and swallowed. 'You're not getting it.'

Alex was not that surprised. He hadn't put a foot wrong in six years, but he was only thirty-two, there would be time. He thought they might get someone in, someone with more experience to handle their crusty older clients. He was disappointed but not devastated. 'Do you think they've got someone already?'

There was a pause between them as Simon lit another cigarette.

'Anyway, how come you know so much?'

'Well. They're not looking.'

Alex sipped his Pernod, with ice, with a slice of orange. He sipped it twice, and a third time. 'What's going on?'

Simon could hold off no longer; he knew that getting him to tell Alex was McBride's way of testing him out, something he just had to get out of the way. Simon felt now that perhaps McBride had just taken the easy way out; it really should be the head of the firm handling these things. 'It's me. I'm the new partner.'

'You?' Alex was unable to speak for a moment; he stared back at Simon and waited for him to go on.

'Yes, me.' Simon looked back at him; calmer now that it had been done. 'It stands to reason in a way. I mean, you're obviously super-amazing at what you do. Better than me in many ways like that.'

'Many ways!'

'Well, I suppose most ways, I guess.' Simon took note of Alex's incredulity and worked hard to not stumble over his words. 'But really, if you're going to be practical about things, of course we might as well keep you doing that.'

'We!'

'Well, yes. The...the other partners and I.'

'You don't think you're going to be my boss, do you?'

'Well...ah...I'd envisage you'd be pretty much your own man. We'd swing cases your way and then pretty much away you'd go, I'd presume.'

'But...' Things were moving too fast for Alex. 'On what criteria do you get it ahead of me?'

Simon knew that Alex was interested in the partnership, but he hadn't expected him to make things difficult. After all, Nicholson, Olsen and McBride was one of the oldest and best firms in the city; people had considered Alex lucky to get in six years ago.

'This is business, Alex.' And suddenly Simon was patronising him.

'What? What about you ploughing into that fence at Beaumont, blind drunk! McBride must have used up half the firm's annual phone account getting you off that one. And a few quiet payments here and there.' Alex had wondered at the time whether they would have done the same for him; now he had no doubt.

Simon sighed slowly and deeply.

Alex's mind raced with things that had happened in the last few months: conversations, little looks between major players in the firm, tiny mistakes that you wouldn't normally expect would be noticed; trying to rationalise the irrational. 'Business, is it? And why wasn't old McBride here to tell me himself?' Alex's voice was beginning to rise in anger and that surprised even himself. He would check that from here on.

'Well, they thought it would be better like this. Congenial surroundings and all that.'

'And so I'd go home and lick my wounds and come back smiling on Monday morning. Is that the story?'

Simon smiled grimly. He hadn't expected Alex to take it so badly. There was an unwritten expectation that any new partners would come from the traditional background of the firm. Simon thought everyone knew that. That Alex had been seen to have his hopes up was very nice, even cute. Obviously he was good at what he did, excellent even, but for partnership? One expected that Alex might start up his own practice one day, somewhere in the Western suburbs.

'So you expect me to come in working like a slave, and for you?' Alex winced within himself at the hackneyed expression he'd used; he had worked hard at his English expression in the last few years. One day at law school he'd described something as a 'cotton bull story' and some of his colleagues had smiled smugly; one had laughed openly. He had worked hard to recognise clichés and to get them out of his lexicon; they were too dangerous.

'Old boy, there's no use getting steamed up about this. Nothing's going to change if you do.'

Already Simon was getting another round of drinks; that would be three Pernods before dinner already, one more than he ever had normally. Alex marvelled at him: he showed no emotion, no guilt; he wanted everything to roll along at its predictable pace and for there to be no conflict. Somehow Alex thought that it wouldn't happen like that.

*

As Alex drove, he went over the story of Themistocles yet again. With hordes of Persians invading Greece, Themistocles had stuck to the most audacious strategy. When the oracle advised the Athenians to seek safety in a wall of wood, the majority had wanted to hide behind the palisade which protected the Acropolis.

But Themistocles had a bolder plan, to take to the water. The ships the Athenians had been building were to be the wall of wood and he said they could win on sea even though outnumbered five to one. They took to the sea, lured the Persians into narrow straits, and democracy was saved.

Alex took strength from this story when he had decisions to make about cases and sometimes about other things; it gave him a confidence in the power of one man. And Themistocles had succeeded against the odds; his mother had been an outsider, not an Athenian.

Alex parked the car in Tynte Street and keyed the central lock into place. His routine was to drive up to North Adelaide and pick up Suzi at the Old Lion or Wellington or wherever it was her crowd had gathered. Normally, he would have a bitters, lime and soda and then one glass of wine with dinner before driving his pissed girlfriend home. Tonight Alex ordered Scotch and soda.

'What's up with you?' Suzi was bony slim, size-A cups. She had blonde hair cut in a fringe and straight nearly to her shoulders, a blonde Cleopatra. She was different from the fuller women most of his old school friends had gone after, and Alex liked that.

'Just feel like a drink tonight.'

'Welcome to the land of the living,' Suzi raised her champagne in salute. 'O, he who is creased of brow.' She frowned in imitation.

Sometimes Suzi's cockiness brought him up with it, it empowered him to come along for the ride. Tonight it was giving him the shits already.

'OK, what's up, driver?'

Alex looked sourly on her. 'The partnership's all over… I mean in the sense that I didn't get it.'

'Poor baby.' Suzi pouted in imitation of some TV bimbo. 'Wanna go home early tonight?' she breathed and put her arm around his waist and brushed her thigh between his legs.

'Oh for fuck's sake. Isn't anything ever allowed to be serious with you lot?' Whenever they'd had little fights, it seemed that sex was all it took to make Suzi happy again; the issues just floated away.

'Death, taxes, hmmm…' Suzi frowned as if she was stumped for something to add. 'Look, you didn't really expect to get that partnership, did you? It was so sweet to see you trying.'

'It wasn't that I didn't get it. Simon got it.'

'Simon! Interesting.' Suzi had known Simon vaguely for fifteen years; she knew what he was like. She'd heard plenty.

'Interesting!'

'He's not very good, is he? I mean, at what he does.'

'He's appalling, pathetic. Weak-chinned…'

'Come, now. But I guess he'd be suitable to an extent for management. Liaison, stuff like that.' The case was closed as far as she was concerned; they could do as they liked, it was business.

Alex was not in the mood for socialising with Sarah, Ally and Rochelle. 'I saw someone I know in the other bar,' he lied. 'I think I'll go out there for a minute.'

'Suit yourself.'

*

In the front bar, the crowd was rougher but good-natured. He ordered beer and found himself tuned in to the cricket like most of the locals. Lillee was still going; rhythm, precision and cunning were his tools of trade.

One drinker yelled, 'Bounce 'im out, Lillee.'

The big left-hander was still there, looking like he wasn't going to be intimidated by anything. Lillee worked away, no bouncers, and eventually got his man with one that moved late.

Between balls and overs, Alex's mind chewed on the problem of McBride, how to bring him down. He wished he'd punched that smug prick Simon in the nose to give him something to show McBride on Monday morning. He drank until he was the drunkest person in the bar and the cricket was all over and the blokes he'd been talking to began to turn away from the screen and relied on their own little groups. If he left now, it would look like he'd been there especially for the game; if he stayed on it would be obvious he had nowhere to go and was desperate for the company of those who weren't his friends.

Alex drove back into town feeling smooth and in control, loving the power and looseness he was finding within himself, driving faster than usual. He had achieved a feeling of not caring about things, which was so unusual for him. He steered his ship smoothly, Themistocles at the helm. 'Take to the seas,' he told himself, 'take to the seas.'

He headed straight back to Pirie Street and had unexpected difficulty parking. He was not used to the new night clubs that had sprung up in the business district. Suddenly a boy and girl stepped out from the kerb and he had to brake suddenly to avoid them. They put up their hands and one cried out, 'OK, buddy,' the other said, 'Sorry, mate,' and nodded in his direction. They had recognised their fault; there was a natural fairness about them which made Alex stop his car and watch them across the street, willing them to safety. His eyes filled with tears for what his life was missing and he crunched up his face and placed his forehead on the steering wheel in anguish. Simon would never have admitted being the cause of a problem and Alex wondered whether he was becoming more like Simon every day.

That's where he'd be in his practice in the suburbs, defending these kids. Probably rorting their Austudy or dole payments and getting into trouble, and he'd get the case. He thought of defending drunk drivers and writing wills for septuagenarian Greek patriarchs. Alex felt inclusion with the two and almost as if he was losing something as they stumbled away into the dark.

He put the car into the nearest parking station and walked back towards his office. He didn't know what he was going to do in there but he had visions of something irremediable; repudiation at any cost. Perhaps he would write McBride a letter and tell him what he really thought. His blue plastic mil key was nestled in his left hand inside his pocket as he stomped along. He saw himself in court, working for a third of what he did now, but it would be worth it, he would be on the side of right.

He stopped before the bright yellow plastic panel of the side door. What would Themistocles have done? In the modern world? In the modern world, he probably would have joined the palisade group because they had been in the overwhelming majority at the beginning; to have gone against them would have been to risk his own survival. The Persians would have placed a siege on the city and he would have cut a deal with them to have himself installed as puppet leader backed up by their military power. It might have been the end of democracy for the ancient and modern worlds put together, but at least he would've been certain to be safe.

They were all just doing what they had to do: McBride was obeying the rules of his station, Suzi was just being what she was expected to be, and his parents did what they'd had to do. But Alex had always told himself that he was different. His first fate called him to a practice in the suburbs, to hide behind a fence of sticks. He called to the doubting voters within him to take to the seas and struggled to win them.

Alex clenched his fist tight and whacked it once, hard, into the plastic-plated door, just hard enough so he could feel the sting of the blow on his knuckles, but not so hard that anything was broken. He looked at this hand, his fingers moving as if they had their own life for just a second, not controlled by him. He watched the fingers slip the plastic key into his trouser pocket; he turned and walked to the nearest taxi rank as crisply as he could manage, his arms swinging rhythmically by his sides. He was the new Lillee moving in to bowl.

Stepping on Seaweed

It was the masthead of the tram that caught him by surprise that morning after. Not that there was anything unusual about him dragging his feet up Elgin Street like he had just got out of bed and was on the way to the shop to get the paper and some milk for his morning coffee at eleven o'clock. Nor was there anything unusual about the sight of the tram clattering around the Lygon Street corner, nor even about the destination painted up on that masthead in old-time thirties writing. But some days things take you differently, you see things you never saw before and you need things you didn't need the day before in quite the same way.

'St Kilda Beach' was what it said. To him, 'the beach' was the same thing as saying 'the past', ancient history. Something he had packed away in a recessed corner of his soul like a condom stuffed in a jeans back pocket – for future use, maybe one day. Anyway, where he came from, someone would think of a beach as something long and straight then curling to the end of a broad, wide bay – gold to white, seared with sun. Henley, Glenelg, Somerton and Seacliff had been obscured in his memory, something wholesome. And St Kilda was the land of the monster mouth and the detritus of debauch, not like a proper beach at all.

But this morning that word 'beach' laughed at him and lured him. The tram groaned to its halt in front of him just as he walked towards it and it seemed the most natural thing that he should be on it. He jumped on board; he took a seat, but not a ticket. He didn't know why he was doing this but he told himself that this would make him feel superior to this stupid town; a tram ride to a beach in Melbourne, quel

laugh. He folded his arms and waited for the pull of the take-off, as if
to say, 'Bring it on, then.'

*I'd always been the odd one. I'd never wanted the beach that much.
Sweat and flies and sand combined. And salt-water in the eyes and gasping
breath at swimming lessons. Ice creams that melted before you finished
them. And seaweed that terrified like fingers from hell, reaching up from
under the sand.*

But he felt a weird stirring when gulls began to appear above the
tram's quaint cabin, about the time the driver turned right at the old
football ground and started crawling downwards to the bay. The air
smelt different. Palm trees appeared and gulls fought over an early
Macca's.

In the light of morning, the fish bars and coffee shops looked
tacked on; they weren't the essence they were at night. Proprietors
stood outside looking seedy and embarrassed, as if they were out of
stride in the sunlight, no matter how many clouds were about. Old
blokes smoked roll-your-owns and stroked their stubble; girls hurried
past – going home or going out, he wasn't sure.

Even the mouth was silly now. Not the spot-on goggling night time
icon, presiding over the mess, but absurd, stuck in a serious grey sky
as if it had been dropped from a lorry. He turned his face away from it
now and shook his head. If they could pull the Magic Mountain down,
they could do something about this.

He stood at the top of concrete steps and watched the jagged outline
of the bay, and the waves and the sand. The shoreline was crinkle-cut
with the horror seaweed, piled in raspy, hard-arsed bunches. Just the
colour of it made him feel gross – gummy russet like the deterrent
shots of smokers' lungs they blurted up on TV screens. Shoals of it
packed the beach as if the hands would grab an ankle and pull him
down to Hades, to the home of the mirthless shades, the place where
to be king of all was to be lower than the lowest slave on earth. He
wondered what he was doing there.

I remember standing on the path above the rocks watching girls, not much older than me, playing with a beach ball. A huge blow-up plastic thing which came up to their waists and floated in the breezes, just like the ball in the Coca Cola ad that played then in the cinemas. A dream, that ad had been, and here were people living it. And closer to the rocks many others sat and bathed in the sun. They massaged oil into each other's bodies. The smell of coconut. When I put my hands to my face… I have it with me.

He made his way down the steps, carefully, his smooth-soled shoes not gripping the sandy surface. His stomach felt bad and he wanted to vomit. His mind gripped his childhood with the desperation of escape.

The radios, all tuned to one station, played the latest songs and every twenty minutes a ditty came over, 'Time to turn, so you won't burn.' And along the beach the chorus of bathers turned in time: the spirit of beach diffused through sound waves; the whole city turned on to the culture of sand and sweat and sticky bodies. Whether you were driving the highway or hiding in your darkened room, it was with you too, and you turned over in your mind to toast your back or front in turn. It had been a wholesome era; a time of musclemen kicking sand into the eyes of weaklings.

He walked unsteadily, the spike-point toes of his footwear more apt for picking mussels from their shells than for making time on sand.

The shoes represent him; they are a weapon. He takes one off and rapier thrusts it at the close air, making sure a mere sou'wester knows just who he is, just who is boss. The other follows and he stuffs his black socks in them and walks on, his feet whiter than the coarse, grey mat that passed for sand.

The beach was an escape, perhaps; but perhaps also Melbourne had been an escape.

Sand in sandwiches and flies in hot tomato salad; beach days of 1979. The rules of engagement: no swimming for two hours after lunch, and then only between the flags, and that means wading too. You can walk to the shop and get an ice cream but that will extend your two hours and someone will have to go with you. You know what happened to the Beaumont children, don't you.

A man jogged past with a dog on a lead and frisbee in one hand.

Why couldn't we bring Flippy? She'd chase the other dogs and there'd be trouble, you know what happened last time, and don't ask again. He remembered: two dogs committing the natural act, or almost, until someone threw a tennis ball, whacking the male dog on the flank, and he slunk away. It was the best thing that had happened all summer.

Until they threw the ball.

'For Christ's sake, Eil, the boy can go in now. He's been on his arse for an hour and a half now.'

'Two hours, Ewen!'

'Yeah, yeah.'

It is not summer now. It is April. The beach is almost dead. It is not school holidays. It is not hot. He gains confidence; he begins to feel that he can walk this beach. The wet sand is in his toes and he crunches little shells as he walks. His crazy night is receding now. Perhaps he can see some reason for coming. A freighter is on the bay and he stops to watch it; to his eyes, it barely moves. The ponderousness of sea travel had always amazed him, how anyone could wait that long to get their goods. Still, they never seemed to lose a ship.

In the middle distance is a girl, a hundred yards away perhaps. Arms over knees, looking out to sea like people do, feet pressed into sand.

He walked on more slowly, keeping an eye on her. She turned her head as he approached, not with surprise at his appearance, but as if she expected him to be there. He came within ten yards and she lifted her head slightly as people do when someone they know approaches and they are waiting to be spoken to. Her eyes didn't flinch, but his looked at her, then at the sand, then back again.

It seemed he was meant to say something. 'You know, you should turn over every twenty minutes, you won't get burnt that way.' He glanced up at the clouds obscuring the sun to underline the irony, but he needn't have bothered.

She jumped ahead of him. 'You just want to check out my arse, I'd say.'

He looked out to sea, to the freighter tracking across the bay, as if he'd find an answer there.

'I'll risk it,' she added, to help him out, to fill the silence.

'Risk what? Turning over or not turning over.'

'I think I'll just sit.'

She was tiny; full grown, but tiny.

He pursed his lips and nodded, 'So what are you doing out here all on your own?'

'Looking thoughtful and feeling vaguely melancholic. A bit like you.' She patted the sand a little away from her, making his next move for him, and he sat down pat like they'd known each other for years. She resumed her thoughtful look and he just waited for what was to happen next.

'You been on the piss?'

The question surprised him.

'You look like you have,' she said. 'I have too.' She stretched her legs out and dug her toes into the sand as if she was doing it just for the feel of it. Her feet were brown, as was every bit of her that he could see. She had the littlest toes he had ever seen. She dug them in and wriggled them so the grains tumbled between the crevices.

Then she sniffed and the edges of her lips curved up into a smile as if to say, what a silly thing to do. 'Doesn't help. Just feel like crap the next morning. That's one of the things they say, isn't it? You know, people get pissed and they say, "I really needed that." It's bullshit.'

She was a kind of girl he never met any more. As she played in the sand, he knew that he would never handle her, he would never use her, he would never confuse love and lust with this girl. He would never use one for the other again.

'You have suffered a loss, like me?' she said with exaggerated seriousness, placing a transparent cloak over her emotion.

'I have, but of my choosing.' He continued, equally formally. 'I've run away from someone, and left her crying.' He sounded like the trite lyrics of the pop songs of his parents; the works of Gene Pitney came to mind.

'Are you a bastard?'

'Yes.' At least he had an answer for her this time. 'Obviously.'

'No, you're not. If you were, you wouldn't be out on this beach, would you? You'd be down the Swanston Street sauna sweating out last night's grog, prissing yourself up for your next conquest. But not you, eh. Here you are, walking along the beach when you've got a million other things to do, wrestling with your conscience. Saw you coming a mile off.'

'So why did you ask?'

'Just thought I'd see what you had to say.'

'Did I say the right thing.'

'Mmmmm.' She looked mock-judgemental. 'Pretty much.'

He thought about this. Perhaps he did have redeeming qualities after all. 'Anyway, I haven't really got a million other things to do,' he said.

'You don't say much, do you?'

'I do when I get going.'

'Come on, then.'

As she stood up, he could see that she was barely five feet tall. She could have been anything from eighteen to twenty-five years old. Her face was cute in a way that could've been exploited, even marketed, but he knew it never would be. She wore no make-up. She pulled out of her bag a tiny pair of thongs and put them on her feet. They had silver tinsel bits stuck on the upper part of both feet, like something a kid would do at primary school or as a lark to fill in time on a long summer holiday. He couldn't keep his eyes off them.

'My niece,' she said.

Oh yes, he thought, families.

'You coming for coffee or not?'

'But you don't know anything about me.'

'I know you're a pretty good fencer.'

He looked confused.

'With that thing in your hand.'

He remembered his rapier thrust.

'I nearly did a cheer out loud when you took them off.'

He looked surprised.

'Don't worry, I was watching you. Like I said, saw you coming a mile off.'

'It was a bit difficult walking on the sand with them on.'

She looked at him as if to say, Duh! 'You should've packed the sand shoes, buddy.'

'I didn't know I was coming,' he said, and she nodded thoughtfully.

She started walking and he followed.

'What were you laughing at?'

'What? Right back there?'

'Yeeeessss.' As if to say, Where else?

'My dog.'

'You have a dog!' She sounded surprised.

'I did. Years ago.'

'You see. You don't forget the good things, do you.'

'That's not all I don't forget.'

She nodded thoughtfully again. 'You'd better come and tell me about it, then.'

He walked along a step or two behind her. She kicked and crunched through loose seaweed without even seeming to notice it. And then she skipped across a foot-high shoal of it like a Roman empire prophet walking on water, her little thongs flicking silver through the sea of brown. He stopped short and watched in surprise; then he followed right after her, not wanting to be left behind, not wanting to go around, his soft bare feet crunching the frizzled hands and liking the feeling as they tickled his instep.

They climbed the steps that led towards Acland Street, her silver thongs leading the way and him holding his pointed suedes, not wanting to put them on again.

He turned and looked back out towards the bay, not asking whether she'd mind, just knowing she wouldn't. She walked on half a dozen steps and waited.

All his childhood memories crowded in on him at once. Searing days at the beach, parents bickering, ice creams that melted too quickly, waiting to swim – the crazy dog. The seaweed sat benignly, almost lovingly reflecting the feeble rays that now crept through the afternoon's clouds over Port Phillip Bay and warmed him through. He tried to remember when someone had trusted him, given something and wanted nothing in return. They climbed the rest of the stairs together.

The Cage

Cecil Parker spent a lot of time with his birds these days. They were his children now that his life was over. He shuffled in every morning with a creaky gait that belied his relative youth – only seventy-eight years, not old these days. The birds were the only thing that kept him alive now.

He would stand with his little watering can in his hand and gaze up at the sunlight shimmering through the ivy he had grown over his cage to keep the birds cool in the summer. He could stand there for hours, talking to them, occasionally trickling water into their little reservoirs, still full from his attentions the day before. He knew evaporation would never take that much, but he had to give himself some good reason for going in there, didn't he? He couldn't let people see him wandering in there for no purpose at all. They would think he was mad.

He prepared himself every time with an old slouch hat and baggy gardening pants and fitted himself with some essential item – his watering can or a packet of seed. He delighted as the birds perched upon him, pecking from his outstretched hand and always flapping their wings around his face; they created such a bustle he'd not experienced since the kids were little and the house was filled with Sunday afternoon ecstasies of cousins, ice creams and kola beers and clamorous children's comings and goings.

Those were the days, before his children had grown out of him.

He grinned to himself as he remembered this, and then he waved his arms above his head to dismiss the birds to their perches and continue with his activities.

Doris had always said it was a stupid hobby – collecting birds and building this great cage that covered half the backyard. Still, it was the only thing she'd let him have over the years. It had kept him out of the way and given him something of his own.

The inspiration for this largesse had come from Chloris, the huge-chested matron from the Red Cross, who told her one day that it was important for a man to have a hobby. 'Especially a man like your Cecil,' she'd added with a canny nod, as if all the knowledge of the world was tucked away inside her brassiere with the floral handkerchief that was perennially produced and pressed to her sniffling nose.

Doris had spent more and more time out of the house before the end. Cecil had thought when he retired that she would be more of a companion. But when he'd had to give it away he found that she spent most of her days out of the house and some of the evenings as well. And she never took him with her.

She said she'd have to be always apologising for him. He was always getting in the way and not paying attention. And people would never believe her when she told them that he had been a policeman all his life.

The weather was starting to warm up now, and Cecil thought it was time to give the lawns a drink. He squatted at the tap and connected the hose and turned the water into it.

The temperature must have been well into the thirties and a late November dreaminess had settled over the place. A dead calm pervaded the atmosphere; the leaves in the trees hardly rustled and even the birds in their house seemed to be taking siesta.

He remembered a day in 1939 just like this. He recalled the tranquillity of the street as he walked home from work, and him bursting with enthusiasm for a new idea. People sat on their porches and fanned themselves slowly and drank lemonade. They said hello as he made his way up the hill from his job at the furniture emporium. He was the junior there and Mr Wyatt had made it clear he had quite a future in it. It was his natural respect for people that showed through. After all, buying a piece of new furniture was big event in most people's lives and they liked to be treated as if it was something important, and that apparently was what Cecil was doing.

But it wasn't the success in his job or even the raise in pay that made that day lodge in Cecil's memory. It was because he had made what he thought was the biggest decision of his life. He was going to join up – enlist. He'd decided to give up his job and go off to fight. Of course, he was pretty happy at Wyatt's, but maybe they would even have a job waiting for him when he got back.

Mum had always had her words about Hitler, but she'd never breathed a word about him joining up – never mentioned it.

He remembered walking up the front porch rehearsing how he was going to say his lines, but he could never remember what it was he had actually said when he got inside. All that came back to him was the sigh his mother had heaved and her turning her back on him for a moment, as if recalling some lines she had already rehearsed herself. He'd known straight away there was going to be trouble.

Her lips drew tightly together and her cheeks stayed tight as her mouth began to move. 'It's not as if I haven't been expecting this,' she began. 'And it's not as if any son of mine is going to get sent halfway round the world to get shot through by some German.'

She'd already thought about it and thought about it plenty, she'd said. And the only way around it was for him to join the police force. It was an essential occupation and policemen were exempt from all expectations to join up. He'd be staying here, he'd be respected in the community and even if they brought in conscription there'd be no worries. No, she said, that was it, and that was final, and no son of hers was going to be shot at and taken away from his mother.

And that was that.

Even though it was over sixty years ago, that one memory remained more fresh and real for him than things that had happened yesterday or last week or at any time since then. Sometimes, he thought about the freedom of the young kids of today. At the age of seventeen, few of them would be expected to do what he had had to do.

So the next day he went into Mr Wyatt and told him that he was giving up his job to go into the police force. Cecil remembered avoiding the old man's eyes in his embarrassment and shuffling his feet on the floor and his eyes moistening with tears.

Cecil was startled from his reverie now by the sound of fast-running water. He'd been squatting there for full five minutes as the water from his hose ran fruitlessly away over the concrete path and sank down through the gravel.

*

That night, Cecil sat and stared at the television. He'd had an early tea. He'd dozed off and woken to see the young quiz show champion led through the sliding panels to the prizes.

He observed the young man now. He was of Italian extraction, with sleek black hair and round-faced with a bright-eyed manner that must have charmed many doting aunties. The young man had such knowledge and such confidence, and he was only twenty.

He thought of himself at twenty. He had been bewildered. They had told him the police force would be like a huge family and that you'd be set for life if you did anything like the right thing.

He'd started off trying to do the right thing. But it wasn't like a normal job where you learnt your duties and you were nice to everyone, and where promotion would come along in the natural course of events. There were all sorts of situations that he'd half expected, that he'd been told about and trained to respond to – but when they came along he knew he wasn't ready for them. As if his training had been a dream that he thought would never really come true. Something would snap into place or someone would save him at the last minute. But it didn't.

The traffic accidents upset him. His life had not been preparing him for dealing with mangled corpses or subduing disorderly or drunk or angry or irrational people and extracting some story that would sound at least acceptable in his report.

So promotions had come slowly for Cecil. It had taken thirty-five years for him to make it through to sergeant, and then he was on 'special duties'. The only thing that had kept him at it was the fact that by then, even though his mother had gone, he had the wife and the two kiddies, and that gave him a reason to go on.

And at the station they called him crazy. He knew they did, even though they never said it to his face. Even when they transferred him to a new station, he could see it on the faces of his new associates – his reputation had travelled before him. Here's Cecil Parker, the one who's soft in the head.

He'd been able to take it until the younger blokes started coming through. Ambitious young officers treating him like a joke – wishing he would get out of the way, retire, go elsewhere or crack up under the strain. Two of them kept pressuring him, knowing he had no influence, no authority.

Until one day it happened.

The funny part of it was that there were so many blokes on the force rigging an excuse for early retirement – and Cecil hadn't really wanted to go when they made him. It was too late for Cecil to make a change. He'd been doing his duty for so many years he hardly knew how to do anything else.

And that was why he had taken up the birds.

*

One thought kept occupying Cecil's mind. The birds became a correlation for his own life and his obsession with them became complete. He spent more and more time talking to them and worrying for them. He extended their cage to provide a freer flight down the yard, but still they were his prisoners.

He'd thought to give them names once. He'd started thinking of special names for each of them, from books he'd read or after people he'd known. He wanted to be able to address them individually, to make his conversations better.

He imagined that somewhere there must have been people who chose. Sometimes people made their minds up about what wasn't good and what needed to be changed, and something happened…like magic. So why not name his birds after people like that?

But names would be the start of it all. Names would make them like people and he would think of them as people from then onwards. And then they would never be free no matter how much they pretended to be. He had a name – Cecil. And he had had a job and he had had a mother and a wife and even two children of his own. And he would not push these birds down that little path.

It began to shame him to see them innocently gorging their unearned bread, their beaks bent like scythes thrashing at the seeds in his hands. They began to anger him. They relied on him like vassals on some outmoded lord. And he reaped from them his pathetic tithe of affection. And here his castle stood. And there outside were valleys and trees, real trees, to nest and make alive with their presence.

They bothered him now when they flocked on him, flapping away and wasting their beauty on him.

*

So Cecil went out to the cage one day dressed in his best as if he was going down to The Parade for shopping. He had to mark the special occasion in some way. He opened the top gate of the cage and stepped backwards across the small lawn to his old wicker chair, not wanting to take his eyes from the aperture for a second.

He'd expected a kind of explosion of birds flushing from their cage, a symphony of beautiful butterflies dotting the sky, circling, circling the lawn in their gratitude and then diving away over the bamboo and the back fence to a gorgeous new life in the trees.

But as he sat and watched he found that nothing so remarkable happened at all. He waited and waited and became anxious for something important to occur. After all, his life had been leading up to this. He was on the edge of his seat, clutching his cane in front of him.

At last, a single spirit emerged and flitted to the red, yellow and green slatted garden seat on the other side of the lawn. It twitched nervously around, dazzled by the light of its new world. And in a moment it was gone, skipped over the maroon-roofed shed…and that was it.

Cecil was confounded. He'd waited twenty-three minutes and that was all he had to show for it. And he was damned if he was going to leave the gate open until morning for them to skulk away one by one like thieves in the night. If they couldn't take it properly, they wouldn't have it at all.

He held himself up by the left hand at the gate and railed at them with his cane. 'You pikers, you weak bastards.' He bellowed at them until the tears welled in his eyes.

Cecil banged the gate and the opened bolt clanked its pique against the upright. It crashed back at him and he smashed it in towards the cage again and again and again. His cane dropped to the ground and he rose to shake his fist at the birds when a sudden shudder of pain ran up his back and spread across his chest and caused him to gasp for breath. He reached out for support and grabbed at the ivy that was beginning to blur and spin in his mind.

He reached too far and stumbled forward, his head belting against the corner pole of the cage as he did so. He dropped to the ground, his body stretched across the opening of his castle.

And the cage door slowly swung open, like a drawbridge lowered, and nudged against his lifeless outstretched boot. One by one his birds appeared at the gate and fluttered hopelessly into the world outside.

The Dwarf

'I know you, don't I?' she said.

It wasn't true except that we'd seen each other around for years. Our town can be like that: the same faces in the same sets of places. Our worlds intersected at the Exeter but there was nothing unusual in that – many worlds intersected at the Exeter. My guess was that hers would have included more lawn tennis courts than mine, and elevated houses tucked away in leafy foothills lanes past which someone like me would have been taken on Sunday drives when a boy, to see how some people lived.

'I think you might, from somewhere in the deep past,' I said, and we found a couple of vague mutual acquaintances and she talked of the old days at The British twenty years before.

By the time we'd finished, she'd formed an imaginary bond of such strength that it would have seemed surprising to an onlooker that we were required to catch up on things that we had been doing recently, even in the last month. Her stories of our past together showed an amoral bravado which was exhilarating.

Jacq was short for Jacqueline. I'd noticed her in the way you would notice someone as beautiful as her. Her long, black hair always gleamed as if it had been washed and conditioned within the hour before she went out. The casual clothes she wore were belied by her perfect hands and chiselled nails, and her pale skin was set off by a nose which was long, straight and unassailably patrician. She would have convinced observers of a complete command of life had they not noticed her pale grey eyes, which flicked nervously around every room she was in, always assessing people, categorising; perhaps for position in her hierarchy, perhaps in fear.

'Can I have your phone number, so I can get in touch with you.' It was her saying this, not me. She wrote her number on the back of an empty Peter Stuyvesant soft packet.

I took a sideways glance at her face as she wrote: the grey eyes darted at me and back to her writing.

*

I couldn't get the possibilities out of my mind. I wanted to talk to her across a table, over dinner, to be seen, to sit in her garden. She had initiated, she had come over to me; she must be interested. I waited until the Tuesday to call her.

She answered nearly straight away. Her voice fizzed along for forty minutes but at the end we had a date for Friday night. She particularly wanted to go to the Crown & Sceptre; she thought it was nice there. I rang off in contentment. I felt like I was dipping into a pool of her: deep, warm and slippery.

But our night out was delayed. By Friday she had the flu, or something, she wasn't sure what. I think the sound of her voice got worse as the phone call went on.

The next day I called and she was still sick. She said she might have caught something from the cat.

I don't like cats much. People used to say dogs are more like humans because they are faithful and affectionate. But cats seem more like humans to me because they'll dump you for a better meal and want to run your life for you and scratch your soft furnishings for you and don't seem to care about it. Anyway, I wasn't sure that humans catch the flu from cats but I was prepared to go along with it this time. We agreed to go out to dinner on Monday.

On Monday I received a message from Jacq saying she had really bad woman's pains and wouldn't be able to go out that night. I took a glass of semillon to steady me. I lit a cigarette, smoked it, and lit another before I rang back. Impressions were ganging within me which gave me butterflies about meeting Jacq. I found myself tensing when speaking to her, but the delays made me more eager. I would wait, I would not force anything; it would work against me if I did.

*

I picked her up. I was on time. The first thing I noticed when ringing the bell was her little painted plaster dwarf sitting on a wrought-iron planter in the front porch. I'd always hated gnomes, a pathetic projection of self-conscious tweeness, but now I picked it up and played along, hating myself as I did. We joked that it was her porch gnome as opposed to her garden gnome. Hilarious. I think it was me who started it.

The house was scrubbed as clean as a dentist's surgery; every pin had its place and those objects which did not have places had been consigned to the rubbish or otherwise expelled. I was awed by the fanaticism, the efficiency of it all.

Everything Jacq did was deliberate. Her face was studied; her movements like those of someone who was carefully applied to an important job, like carrying a piece of yellowcake around with a pair of pincers and placing it carefully in a disposal bin. Every time she spoke to me, her words were the result of some very conscious thought.

'Brenda is going to be there.' Jacq spoke from the bathroom while I admired the décor.

'Oh good,' I murmured. I'd never heard of Brenda before and I hoped this didn't mean she was coming to dinner with us.

'One thing I didn't tell you is that my ex-partner will probably be coming. He drinks there, well on Friday nights at least. I hope you don't mind – his being there, that is.'

I said that I didn't.

*

In town, we walked up past the King's Head, she keeping a respectable distance, no touching, no holding hands. A few paces past the Head,

Jacq stopped without warning and went back to the plate window which revealed goings on in the saloon bar.

'My ex-partner's in there. With some bimbo.'

We paused while Jacq studied his face – eyes fixed for once, jaw clenched.

'Do you think he's fucking her?' She was like a sergeant out on patrol, observing the enemy through field glasses, planning the next move, life and death involved.

'Probably,' I replied, hoping that the outward insouciance I projected would creep into my soul and turn me into the tough guy I knew I wasn't. I didn't go to the window to look with her: I have some standards, or at least that was the way I wanted it to appear.

So we went into the Crown and ordered beer and wine. I talked to Brenda. She seemed to take it in her stride that we were forty minutes late. It was crowded and noisy, lots of wood panelling and chrome. Punk lawyers were wearing white shirts and narrow ties, playing pool and trying to get loose on beer, but the poses they kept pulling showed that they weren't quite loose enough yet. The older ones looked relaxed and ruddy with pint glasses or large red wines in their hands. I got the feeling there were a number of wives waiting at home in the foothills, painting their toenails gold and becoming impatient. Or maybe they were out with the girls. I started to wonder if that's where I should have been, until I realised that I already was.

After ten minutes, Jacq said to me, 'I'm just going out to the loo.' After a little pause she went on, 'You know I've still been sleeping with my ex-partner. Sometimes.'

I shrugged.

She went to the loo and didn't come back.

*

I did see her again that night; finding her wasn't that difficult. Brenda walked with me down to the corner.

'You're not coming into the King's Head then?' I wanted a witness, I was going to embarrass Jacq and I wanted her friend to see.

But Brenda gave me a glance which I now see as pitiful, and hurried off.

I walked deliberately across with the lights, not slipping through the traffic as I normally do. Now was not the time for that; I would be fixed and purposeful.

The Head was scungy in the way that cheaply renovated pubs get after ten years or so, when the gloss is gone from the glitz. Thick crimson or burgundy wallpaper with gold wall lights and carpets with blue and purple swirling on it and more pissed office workers still not home for dinner and kids barely old enough swilling cocktails and bundies and bourbons. The boyfriend obviously had class.

She looked round and straightened as soon as I walked in. It was as if she had been turning around to check that door every ten seconds for the last three hours. For a moment, there appeared a worry in her eyes, the vulnerability. A retina of conscience laid like a golden brick behind the patio of grey ice. But her eyes narrowed when she turned to me – no time for suckers.

'It wouldn't have worked out between us anyway.' She got in first.

I tried to snigger. I sniggered. I tried to look disdainful. I looked disdainful. Suddenly I began counting how many wines I'd sopped up at the Crown. I said something. It had the word fuck in it somewhere, that much I remember.

A funny little mug of a male face looked over her shoulder at me, Hephaistos with his Aphrodite.

And they were gone.

*

I woke up much too early. I couldn't read and I fidgeted from one room to another looking for something to do.

There was beer and white wine in the fridge and for a moment I thought about it. I grabbed a haunch of cooked chicken and bit from the thigh. Meat and grease agreed with me and I seasoned the rest with salt and a little pepper and ate the lot with my hands as I stood at the kitchen window. It had rained overnight, I remembered now. It had wet me as I jackknifed home through the parklands. I had barely noticed it then but I remembered it now.

I went outside and sniffed at the moist, fresh air. The rains had quickly soaked into the earth, so that no pools remained. I crouched before my baby eggplants and capsicums. I had appreciated the garden when I first came here. I liked the way it responded to care. I had kept company with rejection before and I knew that those feelings will eat into your soul and if you leave them long enough they will stay in your bloodstream forever. I had to get it out of me.

I turned back inside. In my printer was a letter I had written the night before. I was not going to be brushed aside any more. I glanced at the text and noticed '…never in my life have I…' and at the conclusion the words '…a bottom feeder, a pig.' I would read no more, I could change nothing, I would act now.

By eight o'clock on Saturday morning, the letter was in her letterbox and it was with relief that I lay back in bed and began the long wait for her reply.

*

By Monday, sufficient time had elapsed for her to have received my letter, composed her reply and gotten it into the post any time before Sunday so that it could be in my box on Monday morning.

By Wednesday, I began to realise that something had gone terribly wrong. Had she received my letter she would have replied by now, surely. She might have called to apologise and to invite me to that dinner which we hadn't gotten around to before. It might be that she had called already and left a message but my answering machine had not worked properly. That had happened last summer one time and had caused me some problems. I wasn't going to let a machine make trouble for me this time. I was determined to conquer my reserve and to do something.

Of course, it could be that the letter had been crunched down under the other junk mail that comes in. I didn't drop the letter there until Saturday morning. She wouldn't have been expecting anything on a Saturday because there aren't any regular deliveries then, nor on Sunday. She mightn't have checked the box until Monday, by which time there could have been any number of deliveries of K-Mart brochures and offers of no obligation valuation. She could've picked the whole lot up and thrown it out with my letter included. Even more likely…what if the postie came along and placed the other letters and bills on top of the junk mail? Wouldn't you then take the mail off the top, leaving all that wretched advertising material and also my love letter underneath?

I decided to call her. Not to speak to her, of course, that would be too crude. I would just listen. She wouldn't know who it was and I would be able to tell just from listening to her voice whether she had received my letter or not. I decided to do it straight away. I was taking action now, not being pushed aside any more. I called the number.

The phone was picked up after only two rings. She spoke the single word greeting, 'Hello.'

I could tell from her cool and even tone that she had definitely not received my letter. Had she received it, she would certainly be affected in some way.

Even though her voice became a little more frantic when she cried out, 'Who is this?' I could still tell from her opening word that she hadn't received my letter.

The best thing would be to go back at night time and put another copy in there. I would use a larger envelope. That way, there would be no chance of nuisance mail cluttering up the box and she would find my letter with the rest of the mail the next morning.

I waited until nine o'clock that night, when it would be quite dark and everyone would be settled down from dinner, but not so late that it would be seen as peculiar for someone to be on the streets in one of the city's better suburbs. It would not do to be perceived as a prowler or stalker.

I parked the car round the corner just in case. It was possible she might have visitors. They could come out just as I was checking the letterbox. It would be much easier to duck off somewhere in that case than to get into the car, start it up and drive off, and if I left the car there she would be sure to recognise it.

I came round to the house. Light shone from the front room, which was the bedroom, and another further down towards the back of the single-fronted cottage. The night was warm, still and humid, and, to facilitate any air-flow which might have occurred, the holland blind had been left one-third of the way up and I could see into the fully lit but empty room.

I quietly flipped open the top of the letterbox. It was empty. Even though it was quite clear from the light of the street lamps and the near full moon that there was nothing in the box, still I placed my fingers down and touched its cool, metallic base. For a moment, I allowed the knuckles of my right hand to linger on the inside corner, without knowing why but for some reason attracted by its coolness and pristine angles. There was no dust on the bottom. She had cleaned it out; she had been out there with a moist sponge and wiped away every trace of the existence of the former occupant.

At that moment, she appeared, moving into her room carrying clean clothes from the washing line and sorting them onto the bed. I could see only her waist and hands but as she squatted to pull open a lower drawer I could see that she wore a black negligée with single straps over each shoulder. With her raven hair and pale and perfect face, she was the most beautiful person I had ever seen.

I crouched down to get a better view. More of the room was revealed and I could see the bottom of her face even while she was standing. There was no question of leaving. Not now. Not now that this had happened.

I realised that I had been crouching there, how long, a minute, six minutes, seven? I had been standing on the street side of the front fence in full view of pedestrians for eighty metres on one side and at least a hundred on the other. I stepped neatly into the driveway, which was covered with tiny pebbles. They made a scrunching sound as I took two quick steps, one to dodge around a small gate and another to step off the driveway and behind a small bush for cover.

As soon as I took my new position, I could see that the figure in the front room had stiffened. The body was taut, listening, still in its crouching position where she had been placing some knickers in a drawer. Then suddenly she tossed away the last of the clothes sorting and started coming around towards the front door.

'Oh, Jesus.' I couldn't stay there crouched behind the bushes: it would look like I had come there with prurient intent. I couldn't run into the neighbour's now because I would make too much noise scurrying around the bush and back out onto the street. I stood up and stepped into the half-light of the gravel driveway just as the front porch light was flicked on and Jacq appeared barefoot on the porch.

'You fucking bastard. What are you doing here?' She knew it was me.

I couldn't run now. I stepped forward and joined her on the porch, with as harmless a look as I could muster. I had never been under more pressure, adrenalin was running through me and my pulse was suddenly pumping quickly. 'I've come to bring you a letter.'

'What! I've already had one of your fucking letters, you arsehole.'

I decided to move slowly towards her, smiling, to put her at ease. 'Ssh! You don't understand. I just wanted to talk to you about what we might do.'

'Do!' She was becoming hysterical already and I couldn't help but look around.

The street was still and warm. I knew now that she was going to admit no fault of her own.

'You don't think we're going to do anything, do you?' She began to laugh, derisively, on her porch, with her smug little gnome sitting on the planter beside her.

I don't know how long I watched her laughing at me; probably only a second or two. I picked up the gnome and pushed it with both hands in her face, 'Shut up,' was all I could say two or three times over.

But the fool wouldn't shut up. She started to scream. She reminded me of Elsa Lanchester in *The Bride of Frankenstein* when she first sees the monster, her face contorted in disgust and fear.

If the screaming continued, people would come running and think that I had come there specifically to attack her, and who would believe me rather than her? It would undoubtedly be noted that I was on her porch rather than she on mine.

I pushed that gnome into her face again, more forcefully this time. There was a crack and I heard her gasp as her nose broke. She stopped screaming. Porch lights went on in the house next door and the one across the street. I heard a door slam very nearby. I wanted to stay and help her. Now that I had shown my power, I wanted to show my gentle side. But I could hear footsteps and a shout from the front of the house next door.

I dropped the gnome onto the red-painted porch and ran. It seemed not to smash until I was already vaulting the front fence. I ran. I ran for a long while before I even turned to see whether anyone was pursuing me. It seemed the neighbours channelled their energies into assisting Jacq rather than pursuing me. Very sensible. I was harmless after all and she obviously needed help.

She would be too proud to have me back now. I ran past my car; I just couldn't stop. I ran until I gasped for air and there was a pain in my chest, and then I ran some more. After I had stopped to gain some breath, I walked for an hour, wiping convulsive tears from my eyes and keeping to the quietest side streets I knew.

*

Of course I still see her now, occasionally, around the place, every year or two, just as before.

Jacqui is a delicately balanced vase of fine bone china, with a single black lily, which sometimes leans too far to one side and which needs to be straightened up from time to time by someone with sensitivity, not rudely jolted by mites like me.

Her nose is perfect again now. I heard she'd been moved to a city apartment with a lockable grille and a security speaker; the family decided that she needed protection, particularly after that shocking incident with the prowler. And her life is as straight as that nose and the pretty bars that hold her apartment safe from the stunted creatures roaming Rundle Street.

I see her around once in a while, in much the same old places. At an opening once, I watched her for a few seconds, a folder of papers in her left hand, her right arm gesturing to three people. As they moved through to the office, she saw me, turning away, half finished glass of white wine in my hand. She met my eyes deliberately. She dipped her head just a centimetre or two in acknowledgement and as she passed by her eyes seemed to say to me, 'It's all right.'

She had exercised her right of rank, her right to greatness, and it drew me back into her with a force like gravity; I was diving into the bottomless pool of her forever and I watered that pool with my tears of frustration and gratitude.

The pictures in that gallery were the plants in her garden, the recessed lights in the ceiling the sunlight dappling through her shade-house, and I the plaster gnome sitting on her wrought iron planter, made smug by association.

I sat in her garden and waited.

The Faith

'For God's sake, don't forget to water the lawn this time, Colin. Those little shoots will fry today.'

The gate clanged metal on metal behind her and her heels clicked out to the Lancer parked in the street. Even before she had settled in the seat, her hand went for the air-conditioning controls. She revved the car as the clutch was still coming off and made a little squeal of tyres as she sped away. And the Sunday morning quiet resumed.

'What a hoon,' I thought sarcastically.

There was nothing Janine could be less like.

Brunch with the girls. Brunch had gone from a once a month get-together to weekly and from two or three hours each time to something that usually lasted all day and from which Janine returned freshly showered and perfumed. But there was no point in saying anything – no point in stirring the possum.

It had been hot for the last two days, unseasonably hot for September. Weeks of drizzle and periods of cool sunlight had ended in a storm which had ripped the arms off trees and bruised fences and cars around the neighbourhood. The old Corolla out in the street had leaves and empty iced-coffee cartons and drinking straws piled up behind the back wheel, giving it an abandoned look. I hadn't used it in a couple of weeks and I decided to do something about that today.

I loved these times after storms. The rain washed all the smog off the leaves and left them glistening. It cleaned the concrete path of any tiny droppings and of the dirt I'd left behind from my work in the garden. Only then could I breathe the air and feel fresh again.

But it was Sunday and the Greeks were out, as ever, flocking to the church up the street. And of course me creeping about the front garden and watching it all.

There was an old man out across the road, fussing around his yard. There was no fence in his place and I could see across the road into his yard, and he into mine, but when I looked over in his direction it was like his house was so much closer than all the others.

I talked to Janine about him once, tried to tell her about how unusual he was, and how he held himself with such dignity that it made you stop and look. He'd become an inspiration to me in a way; an inspiration to keep going but, to keep going at what, I didn't understand yet. But Janine reckoned she'd never seen him. Every time I mentioned him, she just sighed and did something she does quite a lot: she placed her left thumb over her left eyebrow and her next two fingers over the right one and shook her head slightly.

When we bought in that street, I hadn't contemplated Greeks. Their church was a block away and I thought it made an interesting addition to the local architecture. Its two rounded minarets (is that what they were called?) stood out handsomely among the cottages plonked around, and the sounds of children playing in the parish school were not unpleasant. At their Easter, a procession passed right by my door and made a spectacle for a few friends on a Friday night. But of course that was in the days when people still visited.

And on Sundays, for the church, were the parkers. Little blokes struggling with big cars: Falcons and old Valiants. The wives often standing on the kerb waving hands and guiding them in. In and out, in and out. Often they were under pressure, late for the service, trying to squeeze their rig into a parking spot that others had passed up. When I first began to watch, I was waiting for controversy, impatience. I imagined the hands thrust to the skies, the muttering in that foreign tongue, the flashing looks that said too much about the past and guilt and disappointment.

But it was me who was disappointed, pretty well. They took their time but they got there, the two of them. And then they buttoned up their coats and headed off without a word. And me looking after them, without a word, wondering.

The old man across the road was watching me more closely than usual today. He was watching with interest and without concealment of it. For a man in his seventies, he was still tall, and he held himself erect and with a dignity I had often admired. He looked stylish in his black beret and large gunmetal-grey jumper that fitted over a black T-shirt and could not conceal that he retained, for all his years, a powerful pair of shoulders and a solid chest. He had never spoken to me but he had watched me a great deal.

Have you ever been in a zoo and watched a primate in a cage that gazed back at you in a fixed and insolent way that said, 'I know I am caged up and you are not but if your protectors had not invented bars I know who would be running from whom.' I watched the backs of the hunched-up Greek couple. I looked back and he was still watching.

He said one word, in an even tone, not meant to offend. 'Wogs.' As if it was a statement of fact; as if it was something that he knew I knew, or thought I thought. And then he gestured to me across the street. His right hand stretched out and he drew his fingers back towards himself.

When he spoke, I would not have been surprised if he spoke the one word command, 'Come,' so filled with alacrity did he seem and so certain of success. 'You can wash your hands inside.' And then he turned and without looking back he began to walk slowly across his little lawn towards the side of the house.

And I followed after him as in a dream. Were I to disobey, what would his look have said the next time our gazes met across the street?

At the back of the house, there was a little laundry and I found him at the basin there. He was washing up with a square block of crude, cream-coloured soap, a kind I hadn't seen in decades.

'Ah,' he said with slight surprise and a little pleasure in his voice. 'So you decided to come.' His manner was different now. He was charming, a host, and he slipped into deferential manners with a familiar pleasure, like a man putting on a comfortable jacket; but still there was a distant mockery in his tone.

'Coffee?' he asked when I had washed up. 'So what do you think of the wogs, then?'

I barely knew what to say at such short notice. Surely he couldn't want a proper answer. 'Well, they certainly can't park cars.'

He maintained the smile on his face but I knew I'd been judged for my lameness and flippancy.

'This much I have observed is true,' he said with exaggerated deliberation, and the look he gave me was fixed but was full of understanding and pity. 'I admire them,' he said after a pause. 'In a way. I've thought about it for many years.'

He paused for a moment and I listened to the perfect silence of the house; there was not even a clock ticking. It was as if time didn't exist in this place; as if the seasons had been suspended and I was standing in a heaven of poise and balance.

'I think it's their sense of duty which attracts me. They have a faith. I'm not sure yet whether it's spiritual or corporeal, their faith. But there's plenty of time for that.'

I began to consider these words and what relation they might have to me, or what meaning they might have for him, but he smiled again.

'Come, look at my garden.'

It was not a request but a gently put requirement. And stepping down from the patio was like descending into the Garden of Eden.

His pergola had been colonised by a meandering and drooping vine which was still clinging to its autumn leaves with a tenacity that seemed to speak of its pride in being the last in the world to let them go. The effect of this shimmering, golden aureole was liberating and entrancing. I felt lighter than I had been in months, perhaps in years, and when I stepped down into that magic garden it was as if the troubles of those years had never been.

On the left was an olive tree, still heavy with succulent kalamatas. And on the right a lemon, rounded Lisbons bright and jolly against the sun. And at the back, most remarkably, a peach tree heavy with fruit as if in high summer. I looked down and at my feet a happy little terrier yapped, and I picked him up and patted him while I looked around me. And I never pick up dogs.

And then I noticed, in the gaps between the trees where the sun peeked through, spinach and snow peas, carrots and parsnips, and summer capsicums and eggplants magically showing with beads of moisture as if they had just been sprayed at the fruit shop. And between them a mulch of leaves and cuttings teeming with worms and tiny spiders pecked at by cheeky little wagtails, snacking and sunning themselves, pert and pleased.

'Your coffee is ready,' and the old man beckoned me over to a table and two chairs set and ready.

On my side of the table was a spiral-bound writing pad, its cover folded over to reveal the pristine opening page. Next to it lay a brand new Uniball pen, with the click top and the clear barrel moulded to a subtle triangle; remarkably, my favourite type.

A steaming cup was set down before me. I felt its warmth in my fingers and in my bloodstream. I took one sip and placed the mug back down and immediately began to scratch out my repentance.

I began to write in a fever, with long, flowing sentences that exorcised every nasty and belittling thought that I had ever had. People had told me once or twice that I was like a saint. This always confused me, because I knew that my thoughts had not been pure. But now I laid down all my sins and knew that I could start again. This was day one.

By the time I looked up from my work, shadows had begun to close in on my friend's back yard. My cup had disappeared and the old man appeared now with my jacket.

'Janine will be concerned,' he nudged me and I responded.

'Yes, of course,' I said, or thought, I'm not sure which. And as I walked back over that road I felt so different, I felt so certain. I felt like I had not since I was nineteen years old and had not tried and failed at things.

In the next few weeks, life changed considerably for me. I had a lot of work to do, of course. That night I walked straight through the house and out to the shed and grabbed the pickaxe and thwacked it straight into the ground underneath the bottlebrush that had been there the last five years. Useless thing, a present from my mother. It took me ten minutes of struggle, but ten minutes only, and the brute was out. I chucked it under the carport to dry out for the fire; under my new regime, nothing was to be wasted. In my stroke of triumph, I looked up to see Janine standing at the back door just looking, saying nothing.

But I was not going to worry, not this time. You can change your life. All the great people say it. 'If there's something you really want to do, just go for it. You'll get there.' I'd never accepted that before, but that was in my negative period. The next day I would go down to Bunnings and buy myself an olive tree, a kalamata, that would be my symbol, my flagship. A lemon too, of course, and then some seedlings. Or should I grow from seed? Eggplant, capsicum, borlotti beans and corn, some spinach first.

With so many jobs in my mind at one time, I went inside to make a list. Janine was sitting at the kitchen table, looking pinched and nervous. But I didn't care. Suddenly I had too much to do, and now I had a leader, one I could believe in.

She didn't stay long after that; just a couple of days, I think. She turned and left, with a tissue dabbing at her nose or her eyes, or both. She said, 'I'd have someone come and take you away if they would.'

'But they won't?'

'No, they won't.'

I was free.

I raked up all the bark chips from my landscaped front yard and put them in a bag out in the street and they were gone by morning; nothing was wasted and I felt a bond with my neighbourhood. It was the strength of karma; you did good things for the world and then the world did good things back to you. I toiled with the pick and shovel and levelled the land and dug into it some horse manure I'd seen for sale while I was out driving. I'd seen bags for sale at the same spot for many years but back then the penny hadn't dropped; now I was involved.

The next day, I stood on the front porch for a little while and looked closely at my work. The lawn seedlings in the front yard had been dug over completely, only good for mulching and fertilising the soil. In their place were a brace of tomato stakes standing sternly vertical with seedlings giggling at their feet. They reminded me of Janine and myself. I had planted a row of eggplants along the front fence for people to look at as they passed by. I told them I'd heard on the radio that if you talked to the plants they would grow better.

One evening when I was walking down to the shop to get some milk for the next morning I saw the lights on at the Perrys' four doors down. I saw familiar figures through the blinds, my other neighbours out for a Friday drink. Yes, of course, it was a Friday and that was something that we used to do. I'd even hosted once or twice. But that was always couples and I suppose it didn't apply to me any more, or maybe they'd come to invite me when I was out and never followed up. It didn't matter, I had no need of that kind of thing now.

And now it's nearly Christmas as I'm writing this. I sit on my veranda and watch the leaves on my tomato plants grow and the fruit blushing gradually from green. The old women from up the street have stopped shaking their heads as they walk past and have given up making that 'tcch' sound that people make with their tongues and the tops of their mouths. Occasionally one of the younger guys bowls along and goes, 'Hey, hey' and gives me the thumbs up. And on Sunday mornings sometimes the older Greeks, when they have finished wrestling their cars into place, will purse their lips and nod very seriously in my direction, and then move on to church, without a word.

This morning, a letter came with an important-looking letterhead. It mentioned Janine's name three or four times and was something to do with the house. Ms McPherson they called her, not Mrs Harrison.

She came at lunchtime today and said I should pack up my things and that the next day they would come with a For Sale sign, whatever that meant.

She said the house was beginning to smell but that it was nothing that a good clean and a couple of days with the windows open wouldn't fix. She said she had something worked out for me if I made trouble. I didn't take much notice, I was too busy watering the sweet corn. Anyway, I think she's crazy. She'd brought a special little box with a wire grille at the front and she put the cat in it and drove away. She didn't squeal her tyres this time.

I never saw the old man again. He must have been visiting from another state, or minding someone's house for them. Still, he gave me the faith, and I'll never forget him for it.

The Lover and the Returned Man

'So I'm not going to go out with either of you.'

The words came down on him with the firmness and irreversibility of a laying on of hands. A shroud of silence settled on him and held his thoughts close; he heard her words and then her pause. Murmuring, slow traffic made a burr of sound that cut him from the world and made him its centre for the eight or nine seconds he had to respond. To take longer would be to admit stupidity, and then the game would be lost forever.

Bullshit, he thought, but said nothing. She would never face a choice of two and take neither. He knew she didn't appeal to everyone. Her legs were too thick and her mouth too sharp to be able to take any man she wanted; she'd had to learn to be practical. Like everyone else, she took what she could get.

The grass on North Terrace; they were sitting; it was lunchtime; a late-spring day. The plane trees let through light that played warmly on them, but did not burn. People strolled quietly, by now accustomed to the warmth of the season, their joints loosened from the winter crunch, their lives apparently at peace. The chosen spot was set back from the footpath by four or five metres. Other couples sat and talked, but were not so close that conversations could be heard. Not a pub – that would have been too chummy and wouldn't have given the right forewarning. An uncharacteristic meeting on the grass was so ominous that the job was half done before it was begun.

It's a time when a man must draw on reserves so deep he's not in conscious control of what comes out. But he must find a comeback line, say something to turn the day. Or he must decide to say nothing, to nod seriously, to turn and walk away, a direct descendant of the taciturn bushman, dignified and alone.

But whichever way he chooses now, each word or act of the lover's will be designed to win her back, ultimately. This is the city. And there is a building and an office and a desk and a telephone, and a girl. And another man. Certainly, he could shout and act emotionally; he could cry and show his sensitive side. But self-pity would be too big a risk. A one-night stand might be won from pity, but relationships are sliced out in the cold light of morning, with clinical, almost medical, instruments of stainless steel.

'He's been overseas for six months,' the loved one had said. 'He'd arranged the trip before we met. I got the e-mail at work on Monday that he was coming in on a midday flight, so I said I was sick and went home to get my car.'

Done.

So his relationship had been a betrayal of another man he'd never known. Well, he knew of him. The returned man liked to hang out late in pubs and wore a sneer, a superior kind of bloke, a would-be intellectual with a routine office job, no better than the lover's. He held himself above the rest, and that was attractive to some women. The sneer came from having tickets in your own lottery, and which you couldn't even afford to buy on your office job salary. And he lived just two kilometres or so away from the lover, almost the same neighbourhood.

Another man – and one he didn't know. He couldn't chase her now. He'd done that for six months already, putting out her fires with other men. Her brief affairs he didn't understand. Why? Why bother? They were starting a relationship. They had everything in common. But now he could see a part of the answer; a map of the route through her maze was forming. There had been more to it all along; it had been dirty pool from the start.

She wouldn't see either of them. He knew that wasn't true. The returned man had claimed his prior right and she had bowed to that. Like explorers staking flags in the sandy beach of a new continent and naming peninsulas for their king or wife or their travelling botanist. He'd claimed injury; he wanted his naming rights and everything that goes with them.

He stood up and walked away across the terrace without looking back. Any words would have been lost in the soft lunchtime air, absorbed by the traffic and the hum of the city, full of normal people living normal lives and doing normal things.

He knew she had a conscience. She thought a lot, she frowned and fretted. His wordless exit took her by surprise.

*

The streets between the terrace and the building were full of opportunities, but he didn't see them. He bought cigarettes at a shop. The girl who sold them noticed his tired eyes and watched the curve of his neck as he checked his change, then left. He saw nothing; his eyes and heart were full of plans, even more than yesterday or last week, but different now, requiring a twist, creativity even.

He thought of it as an unfinished symphony. He knew he could've done better than that as a metaphor, but under the circumstances he settled for it. It was the first thing that came into his mind and he wasn't wasting any more thought on the matter. Nothing sadder than an unfinished symphony. A bad symphony is one thing; there will always be bad symphonies. And great symphonies are the culmination of life. But to establish an opening theme and not to know how it will work out, that was a tragedy. All that promise: variations, the slow movement, a triumphant finale. A symphony, in whatever manner truncated, could always be finished off; there were ways.

*

She boiled the water and placed the little brown testicles of coffee into the grinder and leant her weight lightly on the top chamber to begin the process. Four testicles in the grinder, sliced to bits and mixed up irretrievably.

She poured hot water on and drank the brew. It was Thursday; about time to appear at work for the first time since Monday morning. She walked upstairs and collected up the underwear the two of them had fondled, so differently, so recently. She laid down on her bed, the coffee and pills in her head and the waking up at four a.m. wearing out the whole of her body.

Fifteen minutes later, she rose again and put on the soiled underwear, the clean set dropped back in the drawer. She Murined her eyes and brushed her hair. Fake it until you make it, she told herself, and she caught the bus into the town.

She looked pale and unwell. She drew an outward show of sympathy from her colleagues, and a rolling of eyes when she went out to the ladies' at five to ten.

*

At 2.30 p.m., his phone rang, as it will so often in a day in the accounting area. This time it was the loved one.

'I just wanted to finish what I had to say.'

'There's more?' As if to ask what more could she do to him.

'No, I haven't said everything I wanted to say.'

He didn't answer and forced her to finish.

'Can I see you at the Austral at six o'clock?'

'Yes, all right.' He invested the last word with as mere a suspicion of a sigh as he could fabricate.

*

They sat in the corner bar, away from the noise and the crowds. She didn't tell him anything new. She justified herself. She wanted him to understand. She wanted him to be happy with the outcome, wanted to clear her conscience. She spoke quickly and spasmodically. He was stone, exacting his own moiety of hurt.

'You look tired,' the loved one said.

'Long day,' the lover replied. 'Reconciliations, end of the fortnight as well. You know what it's like.'

*

He took up shopping at the Central Market on Saturday mornings, just to see her. So he could ignore her. She, by brushing up so close to him, would have it all brought back to her: their closeness, how they laughed at all the same things, how they hated the same people, how they cooked together on Saturday nights, drank two whole bottles of wine together and had room for Cointreau afterwards. He would ignore her and she would be cut to bits.

He never saw her at the Market.

*

She rang him up one night and left a message. She sounded bright and cool, like she wanted to be friends. He wasn't going to be friends. He was not destined to be number two. He didn't ring her back.

Two weeks later, he was in Grenfell Street at lunchtime. He turned left into James Place at the same moment her small figure turned right – one of those situations where you almost collide with someone and you both say sorry to each other and smile and carry on. They stopped just short of each other, within touching distance. She brightened when she saw it was him. She said his name and by her manner invited him to stop and talk. He said sorry, as he would to any other good citizen on the street. He carried on, keeping on his way up to the Mall and not looking back.

He was twenty-six years old. He was in love and had been rejected by the woman he loved. He therefore took to parties and to the arms of other women.

*

One Saturday night, there was a party in a small house in Stepney – a single-fronted cottage with the long passageway and bedroom, bedroom on the left and then an open lounge and a crampy kitchen. The backyard patch had space for the hoist and nothing else.

He hardly knew another person there. The party was so quiet that the best opening line was to talk about how quiet the party was.

'Well, it's a pretty small place, but you could still swing at cat in here,' he'd said.

'If you tucked your elbow in you'd make it easy,' she'd replied.

She worked in an aged care home. She wasn't smartly dressed. Her hair was cut in a grade from her fringe, which dropped to cover her ears and joined at the bottom of her nape. This hadn't been fashionable since Helen Reddy was big. She wasn't pretty but her face was regular except for an extraordinary scar, which tyrannised her left side. It came across her eyebrow from over her left temple and when it hit her cheek it angled back towards her jaw as if a brick had smacked her flush across the eye.

Five feet two and tough as boots, but he guessed she had to be. A face like that would have made life hard in the suburbs. But she made him think of the loved one. From the neck down, it could have been her. Just slightly stocky in her legs, and overall she was neat, precise and trim.

She was not as drunk as him and she drove them both home. After the next morning, he never saw her again.

*

On the Tuesday night, the phone rang. It was the loved one again, and she wanted to come and see him. This time he couldn't say no. Not answering messages was one thing, not talking in the street was another, but this was different. This could be the turning point.

She sat on the end of the bed and tried to explain things again. She talked about the other one and said he was a bastard but she didn't say she was leaving him. She began to cry. They hugged and he kissed the tears from her face; he gently pulled her down onto the quilt, which had warmed the scarred one just three nights before. They made love quickly and she left five minutes later.

*

He'd heard that piss was good for citrus trees, but had never had that confirmed in science. Even if most of it was beneficial to every tree in the world, he knew this lot wouldn't have been. The first stirring as he stood under the lemon tree the next Sunday night suggested a teaspoon of iron filings had been summoned up from his insides somewhere and was to be discharged out the end of his dick. By the time it all burst forth, it had become a cascade of razor blades dumping on to the ground between his feet. The after-relief was almost as purely sexual as that act which had spawned the problem; the scarred one bobbing above him, a demon look in her eye, while he thought only of the loved one.

His underpants were clammy with something that shouldn't have been there. He went to bed in shock and crashed out in denial.

*

He contacted his contacts, just as the doctor ordered the next day. And they of course had to contact their contacts and so on. At the end of the chain was the returned man, the world traveller. In a flat not two kilometres away there sat a man he now had more and more in common with. A bond of disease, and a cup of pills to take it away. A strain passed on by some poor, sad bitch with a broken face. A succubus: a body and a face mask. He wondered whether it had really been her, the loved one in alter ego. Of course, it could have been an Olympian goddess in disguise, the mischievous Aphrodite bringing a message to earth to twist events. Or was it just some hardened reject, desperate for love and comfort, much like the rest of us, unwittingly finishing his symphony for him?

He had a feeling that his work was finished now and that it was the returned man who had to face the test. The returned man stood on his honour and recoiled in disgust. He was too great for infidelity, too certain of himself, or rather too unlikely to risk what he had so hard won. His sneer reached right across two kilometres and fell on the lover's house like a curse, proof forever of the inferiority of both the lover and the loved one. As it turned out, he'd not been infected by the gonorrhoea; doubtless, God had insulated him with a hermetic jockstrap. But the truth was out of its cage and the indignity of a visit to the doctor had been exacted. He'd been reduced to someone else's level and that was enough for him.

The lover quickly gave up standing on his honour. It's like honesty – you can only have as much of it as you can afford in this world. A stand-off tactic has a limited life and the timing of one's run must simply be perfect. He took the girl, inheriting all the problems that came along with her.

The returned man couldn't get enough of standing on his honour. He joined the world of the offended and disdainful. He stopped in pubs alone on his way home from work, always alone, wearing the bloodless peace of the patient man. He drank his beer and looked out of windows, his nose held high as his pinched upper lip worked on his cigarettes. Sometimes the lover came into the pub while he was there. They never spoke.

The lover was left holding the spoils, or holding the baby; his feelings on this varied depending on her daily moods. Months went by, turning into years. They have their ups and downs, many downs. But he does his best to keep it all together; it's grained into him now as well as if it were a survival technique, instinctive as a drowning man looking for air, or straws, or a succubus. And he knows that, with every step they take together or apart, in a flat not two kilometres away, sits a man who smokes and drinks, and sits and waits, the final movement to his own symphony playing nightly in his mind.

The Undergrowth

Neatness had warped Emily's life since before she could remember. It had been her job since she was old enough to heft them to be responsible for the geometrical alignment of chairs in her mother's house. Spice jars were labelled identically and arranged in alphabetical order. The hallway runner was beaten every second Saturday morning and replaced, two inches from the polished wooden step which led down to the kitchen and two inches at the other end from the hallway skirting. There was no variation from these prerequisite conditions. The concept of orderliness was even extended to the garden. Yes, the perfumes from flowers were nice and the blooms could be snipped from their plants and arranged for the front room, but one was never to get down too low, down to that musky, peaty, sylvan scent of compost and rotting pea straw. Stay out of the undergrowth. And this thing you've been trained to do, you take around with you as if it is you. It becomes you, or you become it. There is simply always someone watching over your shoulder.

But one day your conscious mind realises that the person who you think is watching you is dead now. She must be dead because it was only last month that you saw her coffin lowered into the ground, her absolute horror of cremation – incineration she called it with a sneer that left no doubt that anyone in her family should ever fall to such an outrage – remaining steady to the last. And so you are left with your subconscious, the band leader in the back of your mind still orchestrating your movements as they have been orchestrated for the last forty-five years.

Emily had become famous among her students, just as teachers everywhere become branded for their unusual traits. Still, it suited her, this work. She loved it so much that sometimes, when she came to an interesting bit, she lost sight of where she was and who was watching and of the fact that she was paid to be a teacher for this one night a week. She would just stop talking and focus there on the world of the needles as if it was a fantasy, an escape: sometimes only for a few seconds, sometimes for a couple of minutes. It was different there, inside the needles where things worked, where she passed the tiny points so near to her chiselled fingers so many times that just to watch it was a fascinating thing. She never drew a prick of blood, for coming close so often.

But still she would look up with her pleased little smile when her job was complete only to see the stunned faces of the girls around. She had gone too far, too fast, too complex. Sometimes one of the girls would say, 'Could you show us that again?' in a voice that held its reproach out for Emily to see. And she would have to go back to the start and this time concentrate and teach the girls what she was doing.

But the girls loved Emily in a way. Her beige or tan twin sets marked her out as a person from a different world, from another place. She was to be treasured, a teacher whom one could almost patronise. Her manner at first glance was reserved – composed perhaps was the most complimentary word – and she lived within a defined place which she knew was hers, and which involved restrictions which others could not see, but which Emily knew existed without doubt.

But sometimes she giggled at lewd little things the girls would have between themselves, some flirting or worse from Saturday night or an intimate reference to a boy's anatomy. It was as if Emily was asking them to draw her into a world which was not by nature hers, but to which she needed to be taken by the arm.

Eventually the girls got to deliberately peppering their conversations to get Emily smirking. They made up stories, they winked at each other, and egged her on. They asked Emily if she had a boyfriend, no she didn't, had she ever been married, yes once a long time ago and not for very long.

But the girls stopped attending, one by one, as the class moved into the winter term and the nights became cold and wet and they became bored. She'd gotten just enough enrolments to justify the group. Eight. You expect two or three to drop off after the second week. Down to five. But last week only three. Everyone was a bit embarrassed. Three: Jessica, Jane and Sophie.

The desks in her room were always arranged in a neat semicircle and tonight one chair had been left by the previous group poking out salaciously from the perfect form – like the willing nipple on a distended breast was how Emily thought of it. The chair made her think of her mother's breast, ample in proportions but always trussed like a chicken stuffed for the oven.

Outside the window, the first storm after a very long, dry summer was pouring out its tamped-up load on the square opposite the college. It was the first real cold of the season but Emily hadn't even turned the heater on: she knew this would be the night that no one came.

Emily turned back to the classroom, to the nipple-chair. She stopped for a few moments with her hands on the cold metal back of the chair, feeling the chill shaft through her warmed-up fingers that had been rubbed and breathed on and thrust in deep pockets for the last half hour. She leaned forward onto the back of the chair and allowed the cool metal to play on her own nipples, once, twice, three times. She closed her eyes to focus on the thrill of this furtive and forbidden act, then slid the chair into position like a firm goodbye.

Now, not a thing out of place, Emily rearranged her cardigan, she smoothed her pleated skirt and began collecting up her materials.

She packed her things together: the attendance register she hadn't opened, her box of needles, her bag of wools, her sheaf of handouts for the girls. She still copied the full eight, even though she hadn't had more than four students in weeks; one never knows. But tonight not even Sophie.

Emily switched off the lights and locked the door. It was twenty-five past six; no one was coming now. But as she pushed through the glass door at the end of the corridor she heard a bustle back at the other end.

'Emily, Emily!' Sophie trotted up the corridor in her rain coat and her own wet hair.

'Hullo, Sophie,' Emily managed a sad smile.

'What's happened, what's happened?'

'I'm afraid no one's turned up tonight, Sophie.' Immediately she felt cruel. She might have said no one else had turned up, but she left Sophie sharing the blame with the others.

'Oh, but I'm so sorry. Tuesday night is just the best night of the week.'

Emily smiled, 'Thanks, Sophie. Unfortunately, not enough people agree with you.' She felt lame and self-pitying but didn't bother to correct herself.

'I'm so sorry. My car went over a big puddle and cut out and I had to walk for miles and then it rained.' Sophie held her arms out and looked down to show how wet her feet were underneath her coat. 'And I didn't bring an umbrella.' Her face was dripping and her hair was flooded.

Emily smiled and shook her head, 'Here, let's use this.' And she took out the shawl she would have used as an example for that night's lesson.

Sophie gasped, 'Oh no, you can't!'

'It doesn't look like I'll be needing it any more. Any way, it's only a shawl, it's meant to get wet sometimes. Here, let me.'

Emily smiled with pleasure as she dabbed at Sophie's face, holding her steady at the back of the neck as she did so. Sophie's natural freshness was unlike Emily's own Palmolive fastidiousness, and Emily drank it in; her olfactory gift for the day.

Emily was not a tall woman, but Sophie was a little shorter again and she could see into Sophie's eyes, half-closed with pleasure.

'There we are,' said Emily when she had finished. 'Well, I suppose we'd better be off.'

'Emily, I'm so sorry about the class. It must be heartbreaking for you.' Sophie was so direct in her manner that often Emily did not know what to say, so she said nothing.

The door of the building rumbled open as they approached. It was still raining.

'It's gotten heavier,' said Sophie.

'You'll have to fix your car.'

'I think I'll leave it. It'll be OK in the morning. It's a Mini and that's always happening. My dad put a plastic bag around the generator or regulator or something like that to stop it getting wet. But when it's like this it still gets in.'

Emily looked at the rain soaking the trees and the lawns, macerating every pore of every person's skin and every crack in every parched bench whose paint had split in the long, dry summer. She said nothing but felt the dampness of the building behind her, the coldness of its corridors and the perishing draughts that crept from the hearts those within.

'Emily,' Sophie's voice was suddenly more timid, 'can we go to the pub?'

*

'You're not married, are you?'

'No.' Emily balanced a glass of semillon between her fingers and remembered a hot night sitting in a chair on the porch of a shack at Penneshaw. Wearing an old T-shirt and nothing else and sipping cold white wine; together, saying little. Three dolphins had suddenly appeared from the water, making a crescent curl in the moonlight before disappearing completely. It was a brief time; there were few memories left now. She decided that Dennis had been like a dolphin, shining and disappearing forever.

'No, not any more.'

'Ah, I'm sorry.' Sophie narrowed her eyes and shook her head slowly from side to side.

Emily looked at her closely for a second. Her eyes had always seemed very big and warm and dark brown until that moment, but now there was something else she couldn't define.

'Long time now,' said Emily, cheering but looking away. 'Hardly remember. Not that much worth remembering, I guess,' she closed it off as always and involuntarily checked that her top button was done up correctly.

Behind her, she could hear the faint thwock of darts entering the board and the little cheers and jeers of mateship following every one. Next to them a girl and her boyfriend played eight-ball. She smelt the stale, beer-sparged carpet and the distant whiff of sweat on working shirts and, for once, was not repelled.

'Do you like it here?' Sophie asked.

In three years of teaching, Emily had never been in this pub and when she passed it in the street she had glanced in and hurried along. But now she had another strength, the bingo tickets on the floor did not bother her and the roughness of the clientele was almost endearing. 'It's OK,' she said.

'How long since you were married?'

'Oh, a long time. Over ten years. When I was young and skinny. But that's the problem, isn't it? Not being skinny.'

'But you're beautiful.' Sophie drew the last word out in admiration and Emily looked at her closely, seeing in her admiration something genuine, but something calculated too.

'Do you fancy any of the blokes here?' Sophie changed tack adroitly.

'What? Here? No!'

Sophie laughed at the aghast look on Emily's face and Emily laughed too and felt a tingling nervousness run through her.

'I'm glad. They're not good enough for you anyway.'

Emily could feel the effects of the second glass of wine beginning to take. She loved to drink; it was about a third of the way into the second glass that she began to feel it merging into her, mellowing her like an afternoon in the sun reading a book in her courtyard. It was

her favourite way of being and it was something she looked forward
to every night. She had taken to it when Dennis left. It was her single
secret and had become her sex..

'I'm not asking you whether you want another one or not,' and
without waiting for a word of agreement or dispute, Sophie headed
for the bar.

'Perhaps it was just the weather,' thought Emily of her class. Even if
Sophie had asked her, she would have had another drink.

She turned to watch one of the lads lean forward, addressing the
dartboard with his bum out and body tensed. He launched his dart
delicately and she was surprised at the deftness of his style and the
lovely, arcing trajectory the dart made before piercing the board. His
mates stood crowded dangerously close to the board; she was impressed
with their confidence in his abilities. But what if a dart popped out
off the wire and speared one of them? They seemed oblivious to the
danger; she thought for the first time that there must be some danger
in any undertaking of significance.

'I got us a cocktail.'

Two bulbous and brilliant glasses were set down.

*

From the taxi window, Emily watched the night lights on the shiny
street and was pillowed by the fizz of the tyres throwing moisture
against the underside of the car. She could see the bay at Penneshaw
and the moonlight on the tiny ripples in the water and smiled.

She would check her eyes in her compact but she dared not move
because Sophie was holding on to her arm with her head resting on
Emily's shoulder. She'd almost asked Sophie how many other lovers
she had, whether there would be someone else tomorrow night. But
she'd said nothing: there were too many needles and too many pricks,
too many coffins in the ground and too many dolphins shining in the
moonlight to take too much notice of any one of them.

Emily drank in Sophie's musky perfume, mingling with the sylvan scent that lifted into Emily's mind from under her arms like a whiff of that coastline, like a pang of seaweed decaying on its drizzled shores and like a hand reaching up from the undergrowth. It penetrated each fibre of her clothing and every pore of her skin; it tickled between her toes and made possession of every orifice of her body.